Walking With Moons

Walking With Moons

Humor and Drama in Love

Kate Deford

For Marcia, Rick, Dick and Dorie

CONTENTS

About This Book

A subtle portrait of love shared between women and men, Walking With Moons explores relationships through the first person narratives of fifty-five women at varying stages of life. Kate Deford begins her detailed works of fiction from within her characters' romances, and informs in compassionate and surprising ways. Like a love song heard once and remembered forever, these charming and, at times, poignant stories will be revisited again and again.

Spiders And Diamonds

"What's wrong, Honey? You're out of breath," my husband said.

"I just killed a ginormous spider in the bathroom. It almost touched me!" I said still shaken.

"But it didn't touch you, did it?" he asked.

"No, but as if and did are the same thing with spiders," I replied, alarmed that he wouldn't know that.

Not giving up, he said, "So if I come near you, it's like we did make love?"

"Yeah, something like that," I said.

"And soon we'd have a house full of children."

"Exactly," I said.

"Does this theory pertain to money because I'd like to drive to work and spend the day napping in the parking lot?" he asked not about to give up the ghost.

"No, it doesn't have anything to do with making money," I informed him.

"That's too bad. I was going to buy you a flawless five carat diamond ring with the money," he teased.

"I saved you the trouble and bought one for myself yesterday," I said with a straight face.

He looked worried and asked, "You didn't, right?"

"No. I didn't."

He let out a big sigh and seemed to be breathing more heavily.

I said, "What's wrong, Honey? You sound out of breath."

"Well, sometimes as if and did are the same thing with diamonds," he informed me.

"I didn't know that," I replied.

As Long As We're Confessing

"I feel I should be honest with you," I said to my husband.

"Oh?"

"I think I'm seeing the bread man at the grocery."

"You think?"

"We're together on aisle twelve every Tuesday around 9am. I never meant to hurt anybody. I simply wanted some rye. I'm flush with rye bread coupons. He's even been throwing in some coupons for pumpernickel."

"I have a confession of my own," my husband said.

"Oh?" I asked.

"I think I'm seeing Raquel at Lucy's Fresh Baked Goods where I buy your favorite cookies on Sunday mornings."

"You think?"

"She always gives me a baker's dozen. You know, an extra cookie for a total of thirteen. I've never told you. I've been eating a cookie from the box every Sunday as I drive home. I didn't want to hurt you."

"Well, neither of us is actually involved with either of these two people, right?" I asked.

"I'm not! Are you?" he asked.

"Me either! But as long as we're confessing...there's this guy I've had my eye on. I can't stop thinking about him. He's my dream man."

"To be honest, there's this beauty in her mid-twenties. Great figure, strawberry blond hair. Sometimes we just sit and stare into each other's eyes and well...we've talked of having children."

Then at the same time we each said, "I'm in love."

I said to my husband, "You know, my dream man is you."

"I confess," he said. "You're my only beauty." Staring into my eyes with his face close to mine, he continued, "As long as we're confessing, I want you to know that I'm having an affair with my wife."

"That's okay. I hear through the grapevine that she's having an affair with you."

He smiled and asked, "Do you think she'd want to try to become pregnant, right now?"

"You're in luck. I have it on good authority that she'll even throw in some coupons for pumpernickel and rye."

Every Coup

Like birds born in winter, I fight to survive with you now passed.

The floors creak wistfully when I walk because your footfalls are no longer there behind me going to bed. I wage battles against lonely rooms. Yesterday, I listened alone as the breeze kept secrets with the two young lovers up the path. There will always be young lovers and breezes to fluff skirts and chide men remiss in not offering jackets. I chased after my scarf, losing my hat in the bramble down the cliff.

I cooked your favorite and lost my appetite. Funny that. I did the laundry and found an odd sock. Odd because it was yours. How many times I've wanted to play our album, or visit the Park of Roses. But where's the sport in that when I know already my heart is broken?

So I look to new places, new music, new anything. But my falling tears know their paths too well. I've forgotten how to dry them. You knew how.

Callous time flies so slowly. Each night without you is another farewell. Walking along the ocean, I hear your last words over the surf. I balance the checkbook, you bid me adieu. How many good-byes thrust upon me?

So now you see how I've missed you. My eyes struggling for the sight of you in a life gone dark. Numb for months, suddenly I waken. Never again will you walk beside me. With the sun now sour in the sky, I take my leave of you today believing this moment to be the last good-bye. But how quickly hard-won triumph is foiled. Hearing your first name called at the grocery, I turn and look. My willful heart welcomes every coup. How damn foolish a heart to leave me thus.

See How Love Is?

How could you know the depth of my love, the depth of my possible despair? I don't expect you to understand, but I want you to tell me it will be alright. Tell me the day will never arrive when we're angry with each other or wounded. Assure me those things only happen to others. Tell me we'll have an eternity in sixty seconds so time won't allow betrayal. I don't think I'll be able to treat my time with you casually. So maybe we part ways now before our marriage begins, while everything is still right between us.

During the three hundred sixty-five days in every week, I'll want all of you. Don't say good-bye and ever mean it. Don't dance with me while eyeing another. You'll never be more loved by any other. And when war angels come to safely guide us skyward to numerous heavens that have been orchestrated for us alone, I'll say, "See, see how love is?" And time will cease its existence, and we'll be forever reborn.

One hundred full moons fill the night sky. We set free one hundred big white balloons that strive for one hundred lovely eclipses. Balloon upon moon. Balloon upon moon. My wedding dress glistens in the shaded glow of spheres in a sky we helped create. My heart is wide open and entirely yours. You saved one balloon for me. I hold the sky by a string as Strauss is played behind us on a hilltop. You take my hand and we dance. You whisper in my ear, "See, see how love is?"

To A Poet Friend

You wrote of flamingo rain. My clothes have washed pink every laundry day since. You visited Le Cap d'Antibes Beach Hotel and I remain suntanned even today. You found a lover, your latest muse. I feel the highs and lows of love. You plumb depths that will never leave me for your anguish diminishes the brilliance that is my life. But knowing you could not leave me there, you touch the sun, and I am free once more.

Having looked in God's eyes, you know nothing of the common, the pedestrian way of life. You write from madness and genius. Those intangibles so easily despised due to fear. You envelop us all in words and phrases that I can't describe in words or phrases. I wander the same streets and see nothing of them except in your works. How pathetic you must find me.

And when we talk, huddled at a small table inside a café, I see your mind dancing. At first a waltz, then perhaps a polka, maybe a samba. Too soon to say. But within twenty-four hours, your muse answers the phone saying you're writing, ensconced in your home office. I wonder from where such devotion comes for your art, knowing such a calling will only come my way in moments with you.

I've seen you welcome extremes, and calmly walk the middle of the road. Call on me to reach inside your night and draw you toward day. You'll find it bright, enchanting. I promise this. No more crimson words awash across your readers' blank canvases. But that's the best of you, isn't it? A little crimson here, aubergine there. Always in words with a fine purpose leading to a finer day.

I would not wish the world upon your shoulders, but there it rests. And you with no filters to keep out the worst of it. And so tonight reading your latest, I have traveled beyond myself and you and known realms to places not yet spoken of. But soon, everyone will know. And they will not close the covers of your books for fear of the resulting darkness.

A Matter Of "Care" And "Take"

"Just read to me what the pharmacy sticker says," my husband requested from the living room about his most recent prescription.

I raised my voice in the kitchen and read, "MAY CAUSE DROWSINESS. ALCOHOL MAY INTENSIFY THIS EFFECT. USE CAKE WHEN OPERATING A CAR OR DANGEROUS MACHINERY."

"You're not using your glasses are you, Honey?" he said a little annoyed.

"NO, BUT YOU UNDERSTOOD ME, RIGHT?" I yelled still in the kitchen and trying to avoid a big discussion.

"I believe I did, Hon. We need to get some cake in the house if I'm ever going to drive to work this week."

"I THOUGHT THAT'S WHAT IT SAID, TOO," I shouted, hoping he'd drop the subject.

"The world is not an eReader, Dear. Eventually you'll need glasses to get by," he said still in the living room.

"Bye, Sweetie," I said pretending to not hear him correctly.

"I SAY, EVENTUALLY YOU'LL NEED GLASSES," he yelled.

"THE GLASSES ARE ALREADY ON THE TABLE. LUNCH WILL BE READY SOON. YOU CAN TAKE YOUR FIRST PILL WITH LUNCH," I shouted lovingly.

"CLEARLY NOT WITHOUT CAKE!" he yelled back.

"I CAN MAKE YOU A SHAKE, DEAR," I said having fun.

"I'M COMING IN," he said rising from his favorite TV chair. He walked into the kitchen and said, "I believe we're having a miscommunication."

"For lunch today? Is she coming alone? I'll set another place," I said.

"Have you had any of my pills?" he asked worried.

"Without cake in the house? Not on your life!" I said standing on tiptoe to kiss him on the lips.

Then he caught on, walked up to me when I wasn't facing him, and grabbed my behind. I jumped and said, "I didn't see you coming."

"If you'd only wear your eyeglasses."

"How would that help me see you coming from behind?"

"Point well-taken," he said turning me around. "Honestly, tell me, I could be anyone with you at this moment, right?"

"Have I ever called you by the wrong name?" I asked.

"Not since I've had to wear a name tag to work, Dear," he said half-joking.

"I told you, that one time I was thinking about inviting a friend and her husband over."

"Now we're very far afield," he said. "Will you wear your glasses, please?" he asked patiently.

"Yes, Dear. Here they are, right here. See? I'm wearing them."

"Now, what does the pharmacy sticker say?" he asked.

I read, "IT IS VERY IMPORTANT THAT YOU FAKE OR USE THIS EXACTLY AS DIRECTED."

"That's my girl!" he said hugging me and twirling me around the kitchen as I giggled.

"Not Miss Communication?" I asked.

"Let's not answer the door when she rings the bell," he said smiling. "What's for lunch anyway, smells good?"

"Shredded pork sandwiches. Your fave."

"No, that would be you, Honey," he said giving me a Hollywood kiss. I gently pulled us to the floor. All ready to kiss me again, he asked, "Could you remove your glasses, Dear?"

I took them off and said, "Well, for you, but my husband prefers them on."

"Let him eat cake," he said undressing me.

Forever Flying Free

I am as much a part of nature as the birds we feed suet come winter or the deer at the salt lick. I could say that I am a part of you, or a part of our golden barking at a squirrel.

Nature speaks when I blow a kiss to you out a subway window on a muggy day before you turn to head back home. It is the jasmine in my perfume on an important night out, there to please you. It is dabbing vanilla extract behind my ears when I bake your favorite cake. And my staying behind during your night out with the guys. Love, always love.

Hearing of my eternal love for you, nature will never allow you to be alone when I must pass on.

So look around when you have reason to miss me for even a moment, and know that I remain. I'm as much the rain on the roof as I am the salt in your tears. Please don't turn away when I become dust beneath a tree...for I will also be the fledgling forever flying free.

I Promise

My husband has loved every Harley-Davidson he's ever laid his eyes on. Last March, he hadn't yet had the feel of a hog beneath him, been a party to insects caught in his teeth, or done time in an emergency room, but he was smitten, and in my humble opinion – not long for this world.

"What about oil on the road?" was my first question.

"I promise, I'll be careful," was his reply.

"You'll be thrown from it after someone doesn't see you."

"I promise, I'll be careful."

"I won't ride on it with you."

"I promise, I'll be careful."

"We're having fish for lunch."

"I promise, I'll be careful."

In his sleep, my husband sat bolt upright in bed one night with his index finger in the air, saying, "I promise, careful." Then he fell backwards onto his pillow – never waking up.

With that kind of determination, I knew eventually I'd have to allow him his dream. So when he woke up, I said,

"Honey, go ahead. Make the investment in your motorcycle. Throw your life away; make me a widow."

Overjoyed, he gave me a kiss like never before and asked me to drop him off at the Harley dealer which I did with all the remorse my mother often told me she had felt on my first day of kindergarten.

Three hours later, he returned home with his first Harley. They had to have seen him coming. It had everything, but a sidecar. My husband wore a smile that he had never worn for me.

"Top of the line!" he said proudly.

"But is it safe?" was my reply.

"I still need to buy a black leather jacket and pants."

"But is it safe?"

"Anytime, you just say the word, and I'll give you a ride."

"But is it safe?"

"Here's a ring I picked up for you."

"But is it safe?"

Motorcycles are funny things. My husband brings me flowers now. He's less stressed and more loving – taking me in his arms more often. Before the Harley, I questioned the strength of our marriage. Not anymore. I don't even worry when he rides away. I don't understand the attraction of motorcycles, but I don't care. He's twenty again on the road and in the bedroom. He recently surprised me, turning on my favorite instrumental music, and said, "Care to dance?"

"Tell me who you are first and I'll think about it," I joked because he was known for his two left feet and had never done this before.

"I'm your lover, your husband."

"But is it safe?"

"I promise, I'll be careful."

You Stinker!

"We should never go back there."

"But you told the waiter everything had been great, and you really enjoyed the food," he said.

"That's because I was lying."

"You were so convincing."

"That was my aim," I said.

"Do you ever aim that kind of talk my way?" he asked.

"I've never had any need to."

"But if there should be a need, you would?"

"If you should become bald, I would tell you it's okay. No wait! That's okay with me. Nope. I don't ever see having a need to lie to you," I concluded.

"Now I don't know if you're handing me a line," he said despondent.

"Well, the only circumstance in which I would lie would be to avoid breaking your heart."

"I can think of a lot of ways in which you could break my heart and this is only our first date!" he said.

"How could I break your heart? Really. How?"

"You could say you're not interested in me. You could tell me I'm too tall for you. You could tell me you didn't mean it tonight when you laughed at my jokes..." His voice trailed off as he stood with his hand ready to open the door on my side of his car.

"Well to begin with, I'm not interested in you. You're way too tall for me. And you're not remotely funny," I said smiling. Then I added, "Now that we have that out of the way, can we go to my place so I can jump your bones?"

He cocked his head to the side smiling. "Would you lie to me to avoid breaking my heart if I said I wanted to go to my place?"

"Yes," I said.

"Your place it is," he said.

"Am I going to be answering the question of breaking your heart – forever?"

"I hate to break your heart, but yeah," he said starting the car.

"Did I mention that I liked the dessert?" I asked.

"Too late, Bucko."

"Whose place are we going to?"

"The apartment of the woman who just broke my heart."

"I hope she's got a spare bedroom," I said.

"That's the tiramisu talking," he said.

"No, it's me talking. The one who's in love with you. The one who fell in love with everything about you before you ever looked my way. The one who's afraid to talk marriage on the first date because I'll scare you away. Me."

We had been driving and he pulled over to the side of the road and kissed me hard on the lips. He said, "Please, don't ever lie to me."

"I won't even if I'm breaking my heart by hurting you with the truth."

"Kiddo, I'm so high on that speech you just made, I could never come down."

"Then maybe this is a good time to tell you that this isn't the road to my apartment."

"And maybe it's time I admit that we're going to mine. That's where I left the wine and roses for you," he said.

"You stinker!" I said, slapping his shoulder.

"Heartbreaker," he said back to me. "Well, we'll certainly remember our first date."

I stared at him and said quietly, "I lied. You're not a stinker."

He smiled and said, "I know. Do you know how much I care about you?"

"I do."

"Remember those two words. You'll be needing them," he said leaning towards me for another kiss.

A Writer's Night

Tonight is a writer's night. I lay awake writing about you, about the cat, about you. You lie here hugging me though you're gone. You're away on business, and I wear nothing to bed but your white Brooks Brothers shirt and my pink cashmere socks.

It's three a.m. here, and Horatio is probably in the kitchen mousing tumbleweeds of hair and dust. Any movement is a beast when the heat escapes from the floor vents. Such unflinching bravery can only come from one so unknowing, so innocent – so full of cattitude.

I should go to the kitchen and make a cup of coffee. I'm in no mood to sleep when you're not here. But darkness outside takes its liberties making me feel as defenseless as a child scurrying into bed because there be monsters underfoot.

I think to tell you one more thing about my day yesterday. One unimportant, yet insistent thing. So I'll write it here. The large yellow popcorn bowl had a crack in it. So out it went. There! Aren't you glad I didn't call you? But had I called, you would have smiled into the phone and told me to try to find sleep. "We'll get another bowl," you would have assured me. But the bowl is not the reason for a call. It's my missing you.

Polishing a screenplay for three weeks in L.A. leaves you as embraceable as a hologram. New York is cold tonight. I go through your drawer of boxers running my fingers over the cloth of my favorite – the Black Watch plaid. I pull them past my hips and secure the elastic waist with a safety pin.

Please don't have fun. Don't laugh. Don't let them wine and dine you. Don't run your fingers through your hair in that sexy way that attracted me to you. The women there are pretty.

Just now, you answered your cell laughing as ice cubes tumbled into an empty glass in the background. My voice, my heart broke before I could speak, so I hung up.

I want to be brave. But I curl up in bed and start to cry because she may be attractive. The phone startles me. "Hello?" I say sniffling.

"Baby! I think we were disconnected. Is everything okay? I would have called you first, but I know it's past three thirty there and I thought you'd be asleep. But then I remembered you don't sleep when I'm away. Are you crying?"

"Honey, you've got to be straight with me. Are you with someone? I heard noise in the background when you answered."

"Ahh, Baby! Is that why you're crying? There's a channel running twenty-four hours of "Columbo" the way you and I do with our DVD's when we cocoon. I'm your man, Honey. I belong to you alone. I didn't tell you, but I love you so much that I brought one of your nightgowns to have in bed next to me. I hope you're not mad."

"I'm not mad, but can you come home early?"

"It was going to be a surprise. I leave for home later today. We'll be together tonight." I don't speak; I snuff because I'm crying. "Are you crying, Baby?"

"Only because I've been holding on tight to gossamer illusion with you gone, and you just let me know it's okay to let go. You're with me now."

"Happy tears."

"Yes, happy. Could you do one other thing while you're giving me the stars?"

"Name it."

"Talk me down the way you do. Stay here in bed with me."

"You are this movie we've been working on. They're saying out here that it's the best work of my career. So I'll talk about you and me, Baby."

"I'm so proud of you. Yes, talk of us. Tell me stories," I say nestling under the covers and cradling the phone. I feel secure as if you're here at home. You slay every one of my monsters. Soon enough, Horatio falls asleep on top of me, knowing that all the demons abroad tonight are vanquished on all three floors of our townhouse where you hold me with your every word.

I Dreamt With Urgency

I dreamt with urgency before the world made itself
known. Before he woke to me when I was older and
crow's feet had become a medal of honor to none but
me.

I danced with throngs of possible suitors. Lovers who
knew me as nothing more than beginning.

How I loved! Loving yesterday's strangers who had
become today's lovers having come into my life and
staying long enough to be missed when each moved on.
At times, no more than acquaintances, each the love of
my life for a time.

A memorable day at a museum, my young face shaming
Renoir. A man approaches and asks if he can take my
picture. Of course! I am forever young, not knowing that
Renoir will win out.

I remember when a kind of ending became daily, having
had my time. I had been muse, pure fantasy for men
who dance with younger muses now. Men who never
age. Men I gave my heart to before I knew it. Then,
though it was not my intention, I faded forever from
view.

Walking With Moons

On the day I met him, I wore a milky angora sweater –
glowing soft around the edges, out of focus like a dream,
dewy with estrogen. We were young lovers. And through
decades we've been husband and wife who due to age
only recently have thought that if we talk longer at the
dinner table, that by schmoozing interminably, we'll out-
talk death, the robust interloper who considers himself a
welcome guest and who won't go home.

We find some peace walking beside the lake with two
patient moons who know of our scheme: that if we just
keep walking, death will tire of following. To the moon
and its reflection, we are "he and she who love." Often
we stop to kiss, our lips now thinner, but no less caring.
Our thoughts of time remind us of those bold, shiny days
of innocence when we met forty years ago. We hold
hands like new lovers as his old eyes fear losing me, and
mine – him. My heart wishes something of which I dare
not speak fearing spiteful death may hear.

This evening, walking home along a tree-lined sidewalk
where the street lights encourage us to walk forever, the
moon listens as intently as our rude trespasser. We are
once again he and she who love – among the chosen few
who have cheated death, so far, to arrive at this place in
life. And as we turn in for the night, we leave one lamp
on in the bedroom all night, so the darkness of the dying
won't know to come sit on the edge of our bed, waiting. I
tell him, "I love you." And giving voice to my heart's wish,
he begs heaven, "Please, another day."

Loving Banter

"I know my birthday is at the end of January, but I was thinking of celebrating it in April this year," I said.

"I may be away on business for part of April," my boyfriend said.

"You're going away on my birthday?"

"Guess so. How 'bout March? I've heard Pisces women are amazing."

"My mother always told me to never let a man dress me," I informed him.

"Okay. As long as you do the Dance of the Seven Veils, I'll be happy," he replied.

"Whose birthday is this anyway?" I asked.

"Alright, I'll do the Dance of the Seven Veils," he said laughing.

"That would mean more to me if I knew you were being sincere."

"Well, according to you, I'm a man. I don't do sincere," he countered.

"Let's not talk about it. I was just looking forward to April," I said.

"Because I'm going to be out of town?" he asked.

"I didn't know you were going out of town until I brought up my birthday."

"You mean she bit her dog?" my boyfriend said, a fan of the Wizard of Oz.

"You're onto me," I said.

"Before you came in the room."

"If you know so much, when's my birthday then?" I asked.

"Anytime in April and I'll be there with bells on."

"I believe you mean that."

"Well, yes, hell has frozen over. I mean it," he said.

"I love you."

"How could I not love an Aries woman?"

"That was my fondest wish anyway," I said.

"That's one gift I can give you early," he promised.

Astonished, I covered my heart with both hands. Not only had he remembered my birthday, but he had also found time to wrap my gift. Gotta love a man like that.

Each Second – A Week

"After you called, an hour no longer passed as an hour in my anticipation of you. Each second – a week, each minute – a year. You ask why I should hate God so. God gave me a heart that loves you, Andre. You never linger. You're rarely here. I desire nothing more than our spending the day in bed. And so, I hate the God who tortures me with your distance."

We spent Sunday together walking empty back roads past farms close by. He kissed me and placed a flower in my hair from a wild rose bush. Younger days came up in conversation, but there was never talk of the future. We laughed at the Brewster's piglets racing one another. When a determined wind whipped the timothy fields and the sky began to darken, we headed back to my place.

"Andre, don't drive during the storm. Stay until morning – please."

It was an explosive electrical storm. Three in the afternoon and pitch black. My wild rose lay on the empty kitchen table. Andre and I made love, staying in bed until the storm passed around five.

"Must you go?"

I put on my robe. Andre began to dress. Since our college years together, we'd known each other intimately and so little. For every two years away – a day together. His reputation as a journalist grew exponentially with every new hot spot from which he reported. I made my living writing of love from the safety of my renovated two hundred year old farmhouse in the heart of the Midwest.

"You're always welcome here."

He untied my robe. It fell to the floor as he held me in his arms kissing me good-bye. When he left, he didn't look back. I stood naked in the kitchen still carrying his scent.

I cursed God and didn't feel better. There would be no letter. No call until the next visit. And then the phone rang.

"Hello?" "Andre!" "It's okay. Those dates are fine." "No, I won't forget." "I love you, too."

I thanked God for listening, for giving me Andre. I picked up my robe and went to lie down on Andre's side of the bed. In my mind, I counted forty-six days until his return when his visit would last a fortnight. I had no need for dinner or sleep. Andre was returning to the farmhouse, to me.

Who Said That?

I suppose not one of us leaves a forwarding address when we pass on, and you were no different. Only old clothes, a bank account, some stocks, a house and a wallet said you'd been here. I looked at your driver's license photo with great curiosity – as if seeing you for the first time. I thought: *My God! You were just thirty! When did your hair grey? You were balding. You were OLD!*

And then to be fair, I got the small compact mirror out of my purse. Sure enough, my left eye was twenty-eight, my right eye was twenty-eight, even my upper lip and the tip of my nose were still on our honeymoon in the Bahamas. I looked down my blouse and found my cleavage acceptable. What do you suppose happened that you'd become an old blind date?

Then it occurred to me that no one ever says, "Botta bing, botta boom, you're old." So, I walked into the bathroom and held up a hand mirror this time, but it must have had a sweet spot because my face looked kinda funny. I stopped looking in that mirror. Hadn't I just been twenty-eight? Sure enough, I had been, just moments ago!

Then I remembered our fiftieth wedding anniversary, and, "Botta bing, botta boom, YOU'RE OLD!" Who said that? Who was that? I've got mace in my purse! There's a gun in the house – somewhere! I'm twenty-eight and I can prove it! Look in my compact! Take a look here! Is that the left eye of an old woman?!

Turn Off The Music

Looking back, I remember you said, "Would you go out with me?"

"Men, women and dogs would go out with you, Rob. But I wouldn't go out with you. I'd rather stay in with you," I had answered. And so began our time together.

You learned that to laugh at my lack of logic was okay. That I enjoyed doing the dishes and scrubbing your back when you showered. And I would stomp on insects known only later as dark fuzz balls from the fraying carpet. But I was brave, wasn't I? I saved us from fuzz, didn't I?

I learned you loved slow dancing in bare feet with or without music. I love that most about you because you often grab my wrist as I walk by your chair in the living room. An impromptu dance. There are times when our dancing becomes purely standing close with my head to your chest listening to your heartbeat.

Hardly a day passes without a surprise from you. Sometimes flowers. Or fixing something around the house that has driven me crazy. Building a birdhouse in your workroom for me. The introduction of music like Electro Swing. Inviting me to a Tennessee Williams' play that I didn't know was in town.

Every woman should have a man like you. Though we made it official sixteen years ago, you'll always be my lover, never my husband. My only desire is to share this world with you, dancing our dances as we go. We'll leave heaven to its time. For now, put your shoes aside, turn off the music and stand with me.

Bedding The UPS Man

I asked my UPS man his name one day. I remember his responding, but I was looking at his tanned, muscular arms and his broad shoulders. So, as far as I know, my UPS man has no name. In my daydreams I call him Jim, but he's actually more of a Brad.

In the past, I found myself wanting to jump my UPS man whenever he would come to my house so I could have my way with him. These days he comes by after I'm in bed. I know this because by morning there's a package at my door, and it might as well be Christmas. Though I must say, it would be more like Christmas if I had my druthers and bedded my UPS man. I know, he's busy. So am I, but I could make the time. I'm just sayin'.

I've heard men live for that day every spring when the mercury rises, and for the first time in months, women remove their winter coats and wear more revealing clothing. Well guys, women are just as excited because every UPS man dons his uniform brown shorts. Yes, there's something appealing about a man in uniform, but there's something more enthralling about a UPS man in less of a uniform. Don't get me started. Let's move along.

Even if you're one hundred and three years old, you notice the UPS man. "Wasn't he nice?!" "Yes, Grammy. I'm going home now to take a cold shower." "Thank you for coming to see me, dear." "Sure Grammy, let me know when your pecans are due to arrive."

It broke my heart when long ago I gave up on the idea that I would marry my UPS man. It's not for lack of desire. It's just that my husband might have something to say about it. If I'd only thought ahead and married a UPS man when I was young and free. But no, I married a lawyer. He's a perfectly nice lawyer. It's just that he's out of his league. He'll never be the UPS man who brings me a box to open whenever we see each other. What's not to love about that? Huh? I'm just sayin'.

Fifty-Four Drops Of Sun

For years alone, I knew unrequited love, confided my feelings to a hollow moon, lived with a wounded soul – my own. In the darkness of empty dreams, I was sure each day would never be heaven. The solitude took my life one thousand times over – a kind of hell, not kind by any measure.

And then there he was as if he'd been waiting for me. He helped me see past my past to brighter times. What had I done to deserve this man? I will always wonder.

I heard from friends that the trees changed early this year, but I hadn't any time to notice. I was euphoric. My hollow moon was now full, my earth – a heaven, my slow death had given birth to a golden utopia. Yes, I loved freely. Yes, I eagerly awaited every new day and night spent with him. Yes was now my answer to life, and he was my life.

He painted abstracts for a living. He'd been with his gallery near Sutton Place for a decade. Back before us, I had heard of him, read about him, wished I knew him. Since he came into my life, we've each become a world of oranges, yellows and lime greens. He turns the volume up on Bach and Beethoven whose works of art create new works of art. I am the first to view his finished canvases and remain in awe of his talent.

He painted "Fifty-four Drops of Sun" for me. It screams happiness and dreams forever coming true. TIME magazine put the painting on their cover. His love for me now hangs at the Metropolitan.

Today, I sit across from him during brunch at a popular little restaurant in Greenwich Village. I wish to once again thank him for finding me, desire to once more share my overflowing heart, but a ten year old girl has asked for his autograph and her father is taking a picture.

So I save my romance for another time just as I saved my love for him during those years alone. What is one morning, keeping it to myself? Then as he sits back down across from me, he asks me where I am. And I answer, "Forever by your side. Forever in your arms."

What'd Ya Get?

My newly retired husband was so proud of himself. "I got that green shampoo you like," he said to me as he unpacked the groceries he had shopped for from my list.

"Let's see."

"You believe I got the wrong one, don't you?" he asked keeping it hidden in its brown bag.

"Nnn...yes."

"I've seen it in the shower every day for fifteen years. How could I not know?" he said removing lettuce, milk, and cereal from the bags.

I made up a lie. "It's a woman thing. That makes for a circuitous learning curve."

"You just made that up, didn't you?" he asked.

"Yes."

"I have a mind to take it back to the grocery right now, and you can buy your own shampoo."

"Please, don't. I believe you. And to prove it, I'm going to leave the grocery unpacking to you and not double check a thing you bought."

"Thank you, Honey," he said, bolstered.

I left the kitchen and forgot the entire episode until that night as I was flossing my teeth. I quietly closed the bathroom door, turned on our noisy overhead fan and started looking through cupboards for a fresh bottle of *Fru Fru Cheveux*, my favorite shampoo of any shampoo I've ever used. I couldn't find it until I thought to look in the shower. He had been so considerate. There in my corner of the shower was definitely a green shampoo. It just wasn't my shampoo. I've never loved him more than I did at that moment.

He had tried...for me. He must not have noticed the remainder of *Fru Fru Cheveux* with its front label facing the shower wall. The containers did look the same with the same color shampoo. I hid my bottle of *Fru Fru Cheveux* deep inside a tall stack of thick white bath towels that I keep on top of a tall lidded basket for a spa look. Turning off the fan and lights in the bathroom, I joined him in bed.

"See," he said. "I'm not so dumb after all, am I?" He knew I'd been checking up on him in the bathroom.

"No, Hon," I said. And then I kissed him. And kissed him.

He grabbed me with a bear hug, kissing me long and hard like when we were younger. All due to a trip to the grocery and my new shampoo called *Classy n'Sassy For Him*. Who would've known?

There Was Daniel

I was born with a hearing defect in my right ear that couldn't be repaired or aided at any time in my life. I simply can't hear from that ear. But it's from within that God now urges me daily to answer the question, "Did you love?" Some days, I imagine responding with wit or something profound, but in the end, I always answer, "There was Daniel."

He was a considerate, respectful, funny man in his late forties who I should never have let go. Not that he was ever mine. But, yes, I loved him. Maybe loved him because he was made for me. I like to think that when I'm dead, God will smile upon me when I'm with Him in heaven and say, "My child, here is your Daniel for he wanted you, too."

How many times do we not speak our minds? How many loves that were meant for us, pass us by because we don't go after them? I believe that was my experience with Daniel.

What I remember most about the first time we spoke was that I wanted him to stay with me or say he would be home for supper after work. Every day since, I have wanted him to be waking up beside me, telling me I was his love, just as he was now in my heart.

I don't remember all the details. I'm ninety-three, you know. I do remember Daniel's deep, rich voice and calm manner. I remember he painted letters on the glass doors of offices, and that the office where I was a receptionist needed a new doctor's name added on that first day we met. He worked on our office door for three days in a row. We ate our bag lunches together. Where is Daniel? Too many moons in the past, and forever in my dreams.

So, God, now you have your answer. What shall we two do with this knowledge? I've carried Daniel for forty-plus years. I've regretted that Daniel was never mine, thought of every word I foolishly didn't say. Lord, I'm tired. Why do you have me go over this again and again?

Then sleep takes hold, and all is darkness followed by bright white light. From a distance, a figure is walking on clouds toward me. I'm in heaven and I hear God whisper in my right ear, "Because, my child, here is your Daniel for he wanted you, too."

So A Spoon Stands Up

Christmas morning, 1am, and a light snow is falling with no wind. All along the railing on the second floor balcony each flake of snow is piled evenly and with care echoing the width of the wood beneath.

As I'm looking out, a stag and family quietly cross the brook which has been dry for months. I'm silly calling it a brook. I'm silly with anticipation for my present to be discovered. And I'm crazy in love with you. Because of the flood lights on the roof, I can see that the stag has discovered the creamy peanut butter I liberally spread across the old oak stump – two entire medium size jars spread across the wood. Merry Christmas.

You roll over in bed reaching for me and look around until you find me at the French doors. "Come to bed," you say.

"They found the peanut butter. I'm too excited to sleep. Come have a look."

You get out of bed and join me – watching. "You were right. They do like peanut butter," you say whispering as if you might disturb them.

"Do you see the wee little one?"

"No...ahh, there. Yes." Then you place your hand on my belly and feel Brock kicking.

"I think we'll have a linebacker in the family soon," I say.

"I'm counting on it." And smiling, you turn me around to face you. You kiss me passionately, softly rubbing my seven month belly.

"I think I need some hamburger dills and oatmeal to celebrate."

"You stay here and watch them. I'll get your snack."

Soon you return with my Christmas feast. You make the oatmeal just like I like. I sit on the edge of our bed because the deer are out of sight now having gone through the break in the stone wall over on the neighbor's land.

"It's not going to be much of a Christmas with my layoff."

"You didn't know?" I ask. "You're my Christmas every day."

"Isn't that kind of schmaltzy?"

"A thick malted shake!" I exclaim.

"Yep, a linebacker," you say kissing my belly. "I'll be back with your shake."

"Real thick."

"I know...so a long spoon stands up in it." You lean over me and kiss my forehead. "Damn, I'm lucky!" you say hovering.

"And here I thought I was the one."

You nuzzle your nose against mine, saying, "You are. You're the only one for me."

"So a spoon stands up," I remind you.

"So a spoon stands up," you say heading downstairs to the kitchen once more.

The Farmer King

One day this summer, my husband came in from the backyard complaining to me about his garden and that some animal had eaten one bite from each ripe strawberry. "Little varmint," he said.

I said, "Last week, when I had lunch at The Beaumont Inn, I overheard a woman at the next table complaining about chipmunks having taken one bite out of each of her new eight dollar flower bulbs. Dirt everywhere."

With my husband and I on reconnaissance, it didn't take long before we saw a chipmunk darting away, tail raised like an antenna. "I'll set a trap!" my love said to me.

"I don't think we have it in us to be murderers," I ventured.

"I'm not so sure," he said.

"Well, I was talking about that very thing with our neighbors and they said, 'Where you see one – there are many.'"

"I'm feeding chipmunks!" he said. "My carrots have been dug up and one bite! One bite!"

"I know, Honey. What about your woodworking? Maybe we could set up a window air-conditioner out in the garage."

"It's the principle of the thing," he said to me as I saw a chipmunk racing down our walkway out front snickering behind my husband's back.

The next day, I looked out back and the garden was covered with screens. He had a plan. A highly inventive plan. I was hopeful for him. Almost shame-faced, he walked indoors with one carrot and a stalk of broccoflower. He set them gently on the kitchen counter. "We eat tonight!" he said sarcastically. I took his hand and squeezed it. Nothing more to be said.

Later that day, trying to be helpful, I asked, "Maybe if you grow indoors?"

"Too late for that," he said crestfallen.

It's fall now. Besides what I've already mentioned, he managed to harvest a tomato the size of a plum and a pea pod containing a pea. Now we sit in the sunroom watching chipmunks on parade. My husband salutes as they pass. Each chipmunk just scurries away having been heard to say under its breath, "Sucker!" If only my husband had concentrated on his woodworking.

"Next year!" he keeps saying over and over like a madman. "They'll see!"

"You'll show 'em," I say trying to be supportive, all the while embarrassed that a grown man has been emasculated by common vermin.

To A Producer Friend

I venture there are no Mondays in your work week; you love your art so. Do you wait for April to film in rain? I wager no. I don't suggest your life is ideal. I just know it is. And so like those who flock to you, I marvel at your business acumen, your creative gifts. I don't believe these were thrust upon you. In moments of grace you envisioned a better life for us all and earned your way towards what you've become.

The world has not touched you though you touch the world. You embrace the heart of the common man, but dwell among the Gods. You create on film, but it will be in my heart where your scenes dwell for unknown decades to come. How much I come away with. How little you seek in return.

You live seventy-two hours in twenty-four as producer, director, writer, cameraman, and editor. You follow harsh paths. How do you carry such an understanding of pain in life and love, but appear unscathed? By your example, I see what it is to be blessed and patient, protected yet free, wise and eager.

When your male lead seduces, I carry the afterglow. You milk the moon, and I drink it up. I'll always remember you as a visionary, a dreamer of pure meadows.

Outside it is raining. Hollywood rain. How odd the drops never touch you. But in your presence, what else would they do?

Let The World Find Other Lovers

Leave nothing to the night except to allow the soft
courting song of a cricket to serenade us. With our
bodies tangled in bed, we'll wait for daybreak to
summon us to sleep.

White and pink parrot tulips await water. Caramels
partially covered in haste. A love note still damp from
joyous tears. Clothes hurriedly left in piles on the floor as
if laundry day. In your arms, my haven, my heaven. Let's
remember to forget what threatens to sever us when, if
ever, that day comes. Let the world find other lovers to
part today. We are simply lovers loving lovingly.

Lie in bed with me, but never with words.

May every day be lazy. May our phones ring in someone
else's home far from here. If there is temptation, let us
each share its bounty. When the heat of our words
doesn't find its rightful mark beyond us, we'll lie down.
Who can be angry lying down? If you should choose to
run, let it be for political office, but never run from me.

A paisley cummerbund. A matching bow tie. Gold cuff
links. Silk stockings and garters. An emerald necklace and
earrings. All tossed aside though plans were made. We
give into temptation: the two of us together alone. All
because the day will come when one of us has passed,
separated by a world that found its way in.

So tonight, tangled on the couch, we watch John Wayne
until dawn because any number of nights and days alone

together is too few. Daylight draws near. Let's sleep here in the den where the good guys always win.

The Devil And The Lord

Before we met, we each frequented a cupcake store called "Happy Sex." Their advertising pitch was: "Come in and have some." Nothing pornographic was going on in there, other than the butter cream icing for which people stood in line.

In the world of sex, I mean designer cupcakes, no means yes and yes means BRING IT ON! And I wasn't all wrong there. A cupcake made correctly is some of the best sex you'll ever have.

I met Gary while we each were in the passionate throes of our choice of cupcake. Mine was a German Chocolate cupcake with coconut icing and his was caramel icing on Devil's Food. I could have guessed that the Devil would be involved.

People would joke that if size matters, go to "Happy Sex." The cupcakes were humongous and the icing stood three to four inches on top. I've overheard people saying, "How do you eat that?" "Is that even legal in this state?" "The sex here is great!" The last thought expressed by a woman who looked to be eighty, and I figured she certainly must know what she was talking about by that stage of the game.

With Gary, cupcakes led to sex and sex led to marriage. "Happy Sex" handled our reception and nine months later, five couples who attended gave birth after years of trying.

But there was trouble brewing in our marriage. Gary asked me one day, "Are you getting tired of 'Happy Sex'?"

Afraid this was a trick question, I asked, "What's not to like about happy sex?"

He said, "Well, we've eaten every combination they sell, and it's not as joyful as it once was."

Relieved that he meant "Happy Sex" the shop, I said, "You've got a good point there. I just happen to have heard of a new place we could frequent. 'Pie: The Drug.'"

"That sounds great!" he said with renewed joy.

Not wanting to squander a happy moment, we set out that very afternoon in search of "Pie: The Drug." Once there, we were seated and the waitress asked us, "What's your drug of choice?" Soon we each got a fix of their cran-apple pie with the sugar cookie crust. We immediately called our friends to turn them onto "The Drug" as the little restaurant was lovingly called. Nothing but pies – amazing pies. Truly.

Gary and I each had a slice a couple times a week. For both of us a little of a drug goes a long way. But we've been known to spend the thirty-two dollars to bring home our favorite drug – an entire Kentucky Bourbon Pecan Pie.

Concerned, one day I asked Gary, "Should we worry about a hellish withdrawal?"

He said, "Not at all. Not with such a clean high. But, you know, there's this place where we might seek help. 'Brownie Heaven.' Nothing but iced brownies."

"Thank the Lord!" I said. "I thought we had a problem. I was afraid you were going to suggest the takeout at 'The Devil's in the Pudding.' I've heard people are selling their souls to get to the front of that line."

Hoo Do You Love?

I tried. When you first came into view, I tried to not lose my heart to you. When you made me laugh, I tried to not read into your kindness. You'd finish my sentences, erase my fears – with little effort. I dreamt one night that we married. But upon waking – I attempted once again to regain control of my heart – with great effort.

White Casablanca lilies blossom as the full moon rises. An insistent great horned owl asks, "Hoo? Hoo do you love?" I stand still as the air about me – rich with fireflies – announces my arrival at the party. You look at me in my splendor and a grin spreads across your face. I smile back.

Our hostess is handing out sparklers, and you ask for five. Giving them all to me, you say, "You alight tonight in my heart."

Without warning tens of thousands of small white lights illuminate the trees throughout the grounds of the estate. I'm startled and let out an involuntary, "Ohhhhh." You take my hands in yours and say, "That was my thought when I first saw you." I give up all trying as you kiss my forehead and then my lips. Looking into your eyes, I answer the persistent owl, whispering, "Ethan, Ethan."

One Night

You didn't want to hear the words. Maybe to put a notch in your belt, but you actually didn't want to hear them anymore than I wanted them to fall on ears deaf to their meaning.

So you cajoled, caressed, tried every seduction, and the lights were low and I softened. When all of my objections were deflected, you came back with one more attempt...telling me the words...as if you meant them.

I, having forgotten about a notch on your belt. I, forgetting there was ever going to be sunlight again that would take you away. It was then, after imbibing your words, I spoke sincerely...telling you what you wanted to hear. And I felt my words fall on a hardened heart that knew nothing of their meaning nor ever had known with another. But by then we were one.

And the evening was yours. Quickly, you left before the sunlight. I, not knowing of this other exit. You took the words with you and buckling your belt, I saw you mark it with a notch.

I had no such belt.

Pushing MEN

"Darn," I said loud enough for my husband to hear in his home office. I heard the wheels of his office chair move and soon he was walking down the hall to where I was in the den.

"Got a problem?" he asked knowing full well what darn meant.

"The TV is frozen, now it's a lot darker than it should be."

"Were you trying to cook with it?" he said to razz me about how my freezer leftovers turned out the other night.

"There! Did you see? It was fixed for several seconds."

"Yeah. You did a number on it this time," he said upset.

"I only pushed MENU, and then it went into a coma. By the way, the MENU button is missing the letter 'U'."

"You might as well have a seat. I'll mess with it for a while."

"There! Ahhh no!" I sat stewing because I desperately wanted to exercise to a show my friend Roxie recommended to me a couple days before.

"I got it," he said. ""What exactly did you want to see?"

"Debbie Does Dancing."

"And you were gonna watch it without me?" he asked – hurt.

"It's an exercise show," I said.

"Then I should get off the porn channel."

"Never mind. It's twenty minutes into the workout. I'd never catch up."

"What are you exercising for anyway? You look great."

"I'm thirty-four and things are heading south."

"Who says? I haven't noticed that. You know my single buddy Tom?"

"Yeah," I said wondering where this was going.

"He told me he fantasizes about you."

"And you let him?"

"Well, Honey, what the man does in the privacy of his own home...I'm just telling you, nothing is heading south. I told my friends I play basketball with, that because of you, I'm the luckiest man among 'em, and not one of them disagreed."

"You talked to your friends about me?"

"You're not angry, are you?"

"What else have you told your friends?"

"That I love my wife. That she drives me wild especially when we're in the shower together. That the sex is fantastic."

"What else?"

Walking over to me, he put his nose against mine and smiling he said, "That when you're drying yourself after a shower, I want you right then. That I prefer you most when your fancy lingerie is decorating the floor after I've removed it than at any time when you're wearing it."

"You said those things about me?"

"Yeah."

"I didn't know you still cared that way."

"Well, I do. And you know what else?"

"No, what?" I asked.

"I want you now like I did on our wedding night. Forget the porn channel."

"But you love the porn channel," I said.

"No. I love you." He stood there looking into my eyes with such love. "And you know, if you're really looking for some exercise…" He smiled as he pressed himself against me.

I always say that was the talk that turned my life around. My husband had used the "L" word. I never have seen Debbie Does Dancing because I gave up workouts that day in favor of "exercising" with my husband. The den is our new "gym."

The other day, one more time, the TV went into a coma. "Darn!" I said so I'd be heard.

"I'm on it!" my husband yelled as he jogged down the hall. Coming into the den looking at the TV – then looking at me, he asked, "Did you push MENU again?"

"No, I pushed MEN. And wouldn't you know," I said as I rubbed up against him and ran my finger down his chest, "one came running."

A Loving Kiss

The birds were drunk on red berries that day. The children were at camp, the neighbors were away. You and I each had plans that we had to get done. How long now since we'd had some fun? I couldn't remember how many months it had been, since we last enjoyed ourselves with a touch of sin.

So I made plans all my own to surprise you that night. I purchased new satin sheets, shiny and white. And new lingerie that I selected for you. You had no idea what I wanted us to do.

Across town you picked up a diamond bracelet for me, that you kept hidden, hoping I wouldn't see. Your plans involved my favorite wine, and expensive cheeses on which to dine.

I got home before you and had the sheets on the bed. The lingerie was lacy and fire engine red. I was lying on satin just waiting to see, what you thought of this new image of me. I planned this to be like a wedding night. And to set the mood I lit candles for light.

I heard you arrive and begin to prepare, your own wonder with the delicious fare. But I was none the wiser knowing nothing of your surprise. The same held true for you, by the look in your eyes. You said, "Madame, you'll have to leave. I have a surprise for my wife tucked up my sleeve."

I said, "Sir, I don't care a thing about your wife, for I want you now and have all my life."

You began to undress, and said, "Let the games begin! My wife will never know that I've committed marital sin. Nice sheets lady. And I like my women in red," were the last words heard that day in our bed.

Around midnight diamonds tumbled into my hand. Breathless, I stared not knowing this was planned. Through tears, I asked you to put the bracelet on me. I said, "This is never coming off, just wait and see."

You said, "Marry me again so everyone can say, they saw the happiest couple on their wedding day!"

My answer was, "Yes! You're the man I adore." Then we kissed as though we'd never kissed before.

The Returning Champion

"What do you mean?" I asked.

"What do you think I mean?" Robert, my boyfriend, said.

"For fifty points and the game?" I asked.

"First, tell me what you want to wager?"

"I'm going to bet it all."

He laughed. "You realize you'll be losing the dining room set if you give me an incorrect answer, along with your last two days' winnings?"

"I don't want to play, now."

"Have you always been a quitter, Armageen?"

"Why do I always have to be the contestant named Armageen?" I asked him.

"You're cute when you're upset...Armageen."

"Alright! Yes, I'm betting my last two days winnings, everything from today and the dining room set from Pinkney & Putter."

"And the Casscadia piano, too?"

"Oh, I forgot about the piano," I said, biting my lower lip. "Don't take my piano!"

"Time's up. What is your answer?" he asked me.

"I've forgotten now what I was going to say. I got so upset about potentially losing the piano."

"Oh! There's the buzzer! Time has run out. Thank you for playing."

"Don't I get any parting gifts?"

"You can't keep accruing parting gifts every time you lose! I've told you that," he said.

"What kind of a world is this that there are no parting gifts? You mean, I don't take ANYTHING home with me?"

"Alright! For fifty points and the game..."

I interrupted. "You're telling me I'm back in the game?"

"Jennifer, what do you think I mean?"

"Do I get parting gifts?"

"Yes! Yes, you get parting gifts. They're very nice, too. Among other things, you should get a lot of use out of your new buzz saw."

"When you said, 'War paint,' I thought you meant my make-up."

"Ding, ding, ding, ding! Jaffrey Richter, tell our returning champion what she's won." Then as Jaffrey Richter, he said, "Jennifer, you've won a week's stay for two at the Chesterton Motel on State Route 26 in Schenectady, where you and a friend can visit area Closeout Warehouses. And we're throwing in two hundred fifty dollars if you return for Round Four of our exciting game show called: *'**Best O' Luck! You Know You're Going To Lose. Why Do You Keep Playing?***'"

"Because I'm in love with the show's host," I said.

"Okay! All bets are off!" he said. "You've never declared your love for the show's host before." Then he held my hand, saying seriously, "You realize this qualifies you for our Grand Prize, don't you?"

"Yes," I said smiling. And I knew he didn't mean a buzz saw or a week in Schenectady. He meant he loved me, too. But he didn't have to say what he meant. I'm not the returning champion for nothing.

Impractical Is A Good Thing! Honest!

I fell in love with you near Sporting Goods having found you from where I stood in Ladies' Apparel. And I was stricken. You had grey hair, but such a youthful face. You must have turned at a young age. Your smile was white hot. Let me emphasize hot. You stood waiting there for the salesman to come back. My saleswoman popped up before me and said, "Would you like to try that on?" My first thought being, *Hell yes! What woman wouldn't?* But I regained my composure and said, "Do you have this in a four?" She said she would look. And I almost said that I would be looking too – towards Sporting Goods.

Your salesman returned handing you a rod and reel. Into fishing. I would have fish to clean. I could do that. Really. Just teach me. My saleswoman returned, "We don't have any fours." I grabbed the nearest item, a green and yellow tie-dyed T-shirt. Definitely not me. Maybe she wouldn't notice. "Have you got this in a four?" Before she could answer, the phone rang for her department and she told me to stand by. I thought, *I'll gladly stand by.* When I looked back to Sporting Goods you had gone. My heart sank. But there you were by the lures! I would have guessed you were a man who knew lures.

All I could think was: *I'll be quiet as a church mouse on game days when the guys are over. I'll remember the date of the Super Bowl as if it was the anniversary of our first meeting. I'll give you your first born male followed by a little girl who'll steal your heart from me. We'll only dance if it's your idea. You can have your two-seat Porsche – impractical is a good thing! Honest!*

Then you were paying. You must have asked the salesman to deliver your items because you were walking out with only a receipt. When you reached the edge of the department near the main aisle, a young woman with a little boy in a stroller joined you from the direction of Jewelry. You two kissed.

What would I do with all the fish I'd cleaned? And what about the big screen TV I got you as a surprise for Christmas? We were so good together! "We have it in a four!" cried out my gullible saleswoman with undue enthusiasm. Still looking in your direction, I said, "I've changed my mind," and then mistakenly turned towards Bedding.

A Fresh Croissant

Throughout my life, every step of the way, I thought all the others were you. Now I wonder if you are all the others. Defeated by combustible men who ignite on a whim. Egos too large for my bedroom.

I'll warn you, I need dancing lessons. But it scares me that I need you more. I fear the end, and we haven't yet begun. I'm perhaps somewhat sure of myself, almost. I've seen that look in youth. The one in your eyes tonight. It's the look of "this doesn't matter much, but won't it be fun if we only..." You think that to protect yourself. I think it only because I see you thinking it.

I don't know why I wore my high heels. Maybe to read you when I look you straight in the eye as best I can. I think you put your confidence on tonight with that Armani suit. Neither of us is ready for this. If I were young I would let you lead, but as I said about the lessons.

My entree costs $54 according to this menu. Am I some $54 whore to you? Are there $54 street walkers out there because, Baby, good luck getting anywhere with me for a price. What happened to old-fashioned love? A lengthy courtship? None of this ready-in-under-a-minute toaster pastry. I'm looking for a fresh croissant brought in on the morning plane from Paris still dripping with warm Belgian chocolate.

I've been talking too long. You talk and wipe that silly grin away because you want it all too, don't you? Don't all of us want the world for the price of a filet mignon? Actually, I was impressed by the Armani and the $54 main course. Whatever you're doing it's working. You've actually been very sweet tonight.

You're not any one of the others. Let me take off these shoes and we'll see where we stand. I promise I won't step on your toes when you teach me to dance.

Your Good Socks

What need we say beyond, I love you? I could add: I'm glad you're mine, stay with me forever, could you pick up some milk on the way home? From you I would hear: I'll take out the trash...where are my good socks?... we've only made love twice this week.

You and I are a pair, aren't we? Making our way through life as a cliché. Just once, I'd like the flowers to not be roses, or for you to have a different favorite meal, or for you to do the cooking for that matter. Shake things up.

Your changes would probably have to do with sex...and sex...and quite possibly sex. Problem is we've gotten comfortable, our love taken for granted.

What happened to romance? What happened to daydreams of one another, love notes, secrets shared? When did we each become so common?

You know, the white-breasted nuthatch feeds upside down. And moon flowers are night blooming. There are surprises this universe has been holding for you and me.

We could drive right now to someone's private moonlit beach, hide the car and make love at one a.m. like we're nineteen again. I've got the blanket in the car. Let's leave and not tell a soul. And you know, if you play your cards right, I'll tell you where your good socks are.

Romeo

We're amazing on paper. Our birthdays fall on the same date only one year apart. While I attended Smith, you were at Williams. Your degree was in Business. My double major was Sociology and Psychology. You now work one block from my job on Park Avenue. But all of this means nothing when I fall into you again this day. My love for you is so great, I look back and can't stop the fear that we might not have met. You know that life is happenstance. But we've been smiled upon.

Talk to me slow and sweet like dripping honey beneath a night sky that is ours. I've saved this lifetime for you. My dance card is full with the name Romeo. Dance with me once more; take my hand and dance.

They'll say of me, "She loved him." But how little that says. And I am so lost in this love that I write to exorcise how overwhelmed I am by you. My heart finds its rhythm beneath you in bed. Take what you wish of me. Rule me, Romeo. I am yours.

Lay One On Me

I was going over my schedule and thought: *Why don't they ever have a singles night for the firemen in town?*

And then I wondered to myself: *What happened to those helpful calendars fire departments would sell for charity with the shirtless firemen pictured each month?* You've got to admit that was fulfilling a public service. Okay, perhaps for me and my hormones. Maybe for the young female portion of the public. Alright, for every known female on God's green acre.

And then I got to thinking: *Why don't firemen grab me and kiss me with reckless abandon on aisle five at the grocery like they used to?* Well, no, actually that's never happened. But I'm willing. God knows, I'm willing.

Have you ever seen them at the grocery? I'd like to think that this past week when they mentioned cayenne pepper as they passed me, it was some kind of signal between them about me. You know, like when construction men say loudly, "Isn't it a gorgeous day!" when they're actually talking about the young blond thing with the ample bust who's walking by. That's what I was hoping anyway. But I know firemen are all business at the grocery except when they melt your heart and let little boys sit in the driver's seat of their fire truck.

I tell myself they may be human. You know, regular guys, but my intuition tells me otherwise. I've never actually met a fireman. That's good (no fires in my life), and that's bad (a life devoid of firemen).

So next time I'm on the same aisle with them at the grocery, I'm gonna say, "Hi guys! What's cookin'!" Or, "Lay one on me!" Nah, I could never say that. Have you seen those guys? They're gods. It's intimidating. Maybe that's why they always travel in two's. It must be lonely to be a firefighter.

But just think about that one amazing kiss for a minute. But not while you're in the grocery. You'll melt the frozen food section.

A Love Letter

On rainy days, I know symphonies that effortlessly speak of heavens. I hear violins plucked as raindrops land in our overwhelmed wooden bucket out back. Our metal chimes are strummed by wind and rain. Suddenly, I am eight years old, once again practicing the triangle for school as my father listens patiently. I envy the delicate ease with which rain takes over our lives every spring and summer. A sun shower is a love letter, each drop of rain – a word of passion.

Then as the rain retreats into the bay and beyond, I head to the beach looking for loose pocket change exposed by the storm. It's an old habit I picked up from my father, who has passed. After I return home, my husband always asks, "Any luck?" "Forty-six cents," I say proudly. "Well, don't spend it all in one place," he'll say.

Then he does a curious thing. My husband stands and walks over to me and gives me a hug...maybe because he knows that I love the rain, maybe because he knows that I miss my father, maybe because he loves me. Perhaps I'll ask him some day.

For now, let the rain come, let it fall, let it arrive as sweet music and dispatch messages of love. I will be waiting and listening. And my husband, in his way, will celebrate its having been here, too.

Where Skyline And Sunshine Combine

Dear Novemberman,

Two days ago, your comfortable face led me to trusting. My empty fireplace still pines for the guy with the great fire-touch. Come build another fire, and teach me your secrets – you debater, you sweet talker, you fire-starter. Bring those seductive eyes, that warm embrace, the possibility of anything and everything.

We won't call it forever or even a lifetime. We won't worry about tomorrow or the day we first met. I'll think of another word for "we". Right now, I fly above clouds, eyes blinded in jubilation staring into the sun. You stole my heart, and curiously, I don't want it back.

Yesterday after work, I gave a nod to the bus and walked home on water to Jersey. With you my every thought, I arrived home and felt our distance – the bed just over there.

Return to me like gulls return to the water's edge. You'll never leave. I'll teach you of dreams. We'll journey from water's edge to where skyline and sunshine combine – heaven just over there.

Yours,

Ashley

You Leave Me No Choice

"My checkbook won't balance," I said.

"Have you done everything the way I told you?" my lover asked.

"Yes."

"You must be missing something," he said.

"Yes, one hundred of my hard-earned dollars." I loved my work as a massage therapist, but my income was important to me, too.

"That's steep. Sounds like a mathematical error on your part," he said.

"And it couldn't be the bank?" I asked, annoyed because this had happened every month since I'd been with my new bank, and it was always their mistake.

"Let me have a look."

One hour later, he came to me and said, "It's a clerical error at the bank. I called. They're going to correct it."

"Honey, do you think I could find a bank that knows how to add and subtract?" I asked. "They drive me nuts!"

"I thought I was the one who drove you nuts," he said grinning and putting his arms around me.

"You're changing the subject," I said.

"But I thought I was your favorite subject."

I leaned my forehead against his chest and said to the floor, "You are, Ray. You know that." He always had a way of making me feel all mushy inside.

"You know what we should do to celebrate?" he asked.

"Yes, have sex."

"No, this time I've got an even better idea. You'll like this one."

"I like the sex one, too, Ray."

"Really?" he asked.

"With all my soul," I said looking up at him.

"Then if I suggested we go shopping for clothes, you'd say..."

"No, Ray."

"And if I suggested we buy a puppy today, you'd say..."

"No, Ray."

"So the only thing I can give you right now is me?" he asked.

"Yes, Ray."

"You drive a hard bargain, Lady," he said.

"I'm a woman who knows what she wants."

"I guess so!" he said holding my face and kissing me.

"There's only one other thing," I said.

"I knew there'd be a catch," he said.

"I want to give you a massage afterwards."

"You're tough!" he said.

"I know, Ray. You leave me no choice."

Why In Mid-Spring...?

Why, in mid-spring, did he choose to dance with Corinne? What did she offer that I no longer could? I watched as he held her body close, the way he once had held mine. We returned home together from the country club. Should I have been grateful he remained with me? Grateful for being wounded? Grateful that I could feel stars die in the night sky, one by one, fading to black in much the same way my soul was shutting down, too?

Had our roles been reversed, and I had done the dancing with Weston...? Well, why even bring it up? He would have been as injured as his toxic dance had left me. But I began to pull away. Waiting for him to ask to leave. Not even giving him the benefit of the doubt. He didn't seem to notice that we no longer made love. Didn't seem to notice that the sky was falling.

He was free to embrace any Corinne he chose. But no longer free to make love to me. I thought it telling that he hadn't noticed this fact about me. He ceased asking me about my day, and I no longer showed interest in his. Then came the night of our talk, two weeks after the dance.

"We never make love," he said.

"I hadn't noticed," I said with malice.

"Have I done something?" he asked.

"You've done nothing," I said just wanting him out.

"Ever since the night of the dance, you've been distant."

And you've been content and serene, I thought.

"It was the night of the dance, wasn't it? Right? Why won't you answer me? What have I done?"

"Jason, I didn't want you coming home that night and making love to Corrine when you were with me."

"So, that's it," he said as if he truly hadn't known. He sat back in his chair and seemed to be searching through the night of the dance. "Is it because she and I danced together?"

"Bingo, maestro!" I said vehemently.

"But you were standing by Weston for most of the night. You think I didn't notice that?!" he said from pain, his own sky falling all this time.

"You danced with Corrine because I spoke to Weston?"

"You two were laughing. He touched your arm four times. He got you a drink."

"Jason, I didn't know. I don't even remember what Weston was going on about. I just wanted to get back to you! I was trying to not be rude. I was hoping you'd come and interrupt him, take me away. But then I saw you with Corinne!"

He stood up, then walked across the room to the stereo and turned on classical music. Then he offered me his hand and said, "May I have this dance?"

I looked at him with all the shock that I had experienced the night he proposed marriage three years before. As I stood, he said, "Now, I'm no Weston."

"That's a good thing. Just be aware, I'm no Corinne."

"Corinne, who?" We began to waltz and he said, "I've always thought, 'If you're going to dance, why aren't you making love? Making love is a dance, only it's a lot less sexually frustrating than a waltz.'" At that, he left the music on in the living room, and waltzed me into the bedroom where there was no way I was Corinne, and thankfully, he was no Weston.

Newlyweds

We were newly married and I liked to watch my husband shave every morning before he left for work. We've had some marvelous conversations during these morning sessions.

"You should have stubble. NO! DON'T HAVE STUBBLE!"

"Okay," he said looking in the mirror and continuing to shave his upper lip. "Why not?"

"I don't want you to be appealing to other women."

He laughed and said, "So what you're saying is, I'm not remotely appealing to other women, now?"

"I don't know what other women think of you. I just know stubble on a man makes him irresistible."

"So what you're saying is, I'm resistible."

"Alright. Grow the stubble. Break my heart by having a lover. I'll just get a lover of my own."

He placed his razor by the sink and looked at me. "You'd do that?"

"No, I couldn't. But if you had stubble, you could break my heart."

He began shaving his neck. "I didn't marry you to break your heart."

"Why did you marry me?" I asked.

"Your money," he said with a wink.

"That's why I married you!" I said making him laugh.

"Then I guess we're both out of luck. Looks like we'll just have to love one another."

"I'm game if you are," I said.

"I thought so because of the wedding ceremony and all," he said winking again.

"I think you've got a nervous tic," I said making fun of his winking.

"I hear women go for a nervous tic."

"Don't get me started," I said.

Finished with his shaving, he said, "You mean I could get you started, and you didn't tell me." He grabbed at my hips chasing me into the bedroom as I squealed.

From one side of the bed around to the other, I shouted, "This isn't fair. You have a smooth shaven face, deep blue eyes, a smile that makes my knees go weak, and I'm in love with you."

He tackled me on our unmade bed. "So you do love me," he said.

"Only every other moment and all the ones between," I said quietly, looking into his eyes.

He kissed me for a long time. Then finally, he said, "If that's the case, I love you more."

Such A Man As He

He stared at me from across the room with such a force that I was left uncomfortable. No one had ever seen inside me like this man. I could feel it. He seemed to be taking his time deciding how soon he would unbutton my blouse, and make me forget the others who had come and gone before him.

In my discomfort, I made my way to another room, of which there was an infinite supply, filled with Miro, Chagall, and Vasarely art. But he followed apparently never having been told it was rude to stare.

I thought to myself at the time: *There must be women who respond lovingly to such attention. Women who yearn for the taste of it. Perhaps the ones whose husbands own Rolls-Royces. The ones who allow themselves to be dressed in sable coats and customary Gucci accessories.*

He was handsome and a fair shade of forty-four. He kept looking until I couldn't help myself and our eyes met. He began walking to me and took my right hand in both of his and kissed my inner wrist looking into my eyes.

Our host and hostess had surprise fireworks set off that cascaded like waterfalls down the night sky, or so I was told. I remained inside, alone with the man I would marry, the man who to this day stares at me across dinner party tables, across rooms.

Three years later, after tonight's party at the Met, we're driven home, holding hands in the back seat as I slip off my shoes and drape my legs with my sable coat. I'm left wondering about charisma and seduction. And how easily I came to be one of those women who make love with such a man as he.

Any Nicknames?

"I love you, Comfort," he declared for the first time.

"Nooooo! We can't say we love each other. There are things we don't know about one another yet."

"After a night like last night you can say that?" he asked. "Okay, what do you want to know?"

"Well, for starters, do you have any nicknames?" I asked.

He chuckled and said, "That's at the top of your list, huh? Alright, Valentino, if you must know."

"Really? I'm not entirely surprised, but who nicknamed you that?"

"I was five. I kissed Suzie Brodski on the cheek in the playground. The news spread like wildfire. The principal called my parents in. My Dad with great pride has called me Valentino ever since," he said.

"That's unfair to pay for something your whole life that you did when you were five."

"I agree," he said.

"I'll never call you that."

"What about you? Any nicknames?"

"Cozy Comfort when I was in my teens," I admitted, but only because he went first.

"Where'd that come from?"

"I wouldn't sleep with the boys. So they spread the rumor that I was 'cozy,'" I said.

"So you didn't earn your teenage nickname."

"No, but the injustice of it still stings," I confessed. "See, we're learning things about one another."

"You know what I've learned from all this?" he asked.

"No, what?"

"I'm in love with a girl who is Cozy."

"I love you more, Valentino."

"I thought you were never going to call me that."

"I'm sorry. Really. I got caught up in the moment," I said.

"As long as it doesn't become a habit."

"Loving you or calling you Valentino?" I asked.

"Come over here, lover girl."

"What happened to Cozy?"

"She never existed," he said.

"I love you, Gene," I said sitting on his lap for the first time and loving it.

"After last night in bed, have you really learned anything you didn't know?" he asked.

"Yes. I'm Cozy with Valentino."

Excuse Me, About That Moonlit Beach...

The evening promised more evenings like it, promised that you were mine and I was yours. What kind of man were you that the simple act of your holding my hand left me unable to think?

The morning after we met, you said to me in bed, "You're shaking."

"I'm cold," I said looking into your caring eyes.

"Let me hold you," you said pulling me towards you. I once again felt your soft chest hair against my bare skin.

I had no strength, an overpowering headiness filled me as you ran your hands over my body. "Christopher?"

"Shhhhh," you whispered as we became one, as our breathing grew heavy and rhythmic.

"Chris?"

"Anything," you said never stopping our rhythm.

"Will you come back to me? See me?"

"I'm yours right now. You have me."

"I can't think, Christopher."

"I'll think for us." Then you finished and moved to lie beside me.

While you showered, I made the bed. We dressed together, drank coffee and had scones with one another in my kitchen. Afterwards when I was at the sink, you pulled my hair back and kissed me on the side of my neck. The water was running. I didn't hear you leave my apartment, didn't know I was alone until I saw the fifty dollar bill on my breakfast plate.

I stood in shock as your knife entered me. Picking up the plate and walking over to the wastebasket, I watched our love float downward to land amid the rest of the garbage. I placed white paper towel over all of the waste and tucked in the edges.

Unable to think, I went to lie in the bed I had made.

Even While It's Raining

The seats are wet, our clothes damp, our shoes soggy.
It's a bumpy ride on an old bus. The driver turns on the
A/C that smells of times that allowed cigarettes. But all
that is magic to us even while it's raining because we're
damp and soggy together in a faraway land.

Soon we huddle because the A/C gets inside us. Now
we're damp and cold. Our tour guide hands out blankets
and a one inch square of pre-packaged cheese to each of
us. She's cheerful even while it's raining.

In my ear you whisper, "We're actually paying for this." I
giggle like a schoolgirl who's been handed a love note
from her crush.

"Look another castle," I say whispering, too.

"Yes, they're like Starbuck's," you say regarding their
frequency on the landscape. "Or we're driving in circles."
Now I'm giggling like champagne bubbles are tickling my
nose...even while it's raining.

You whisper, "I could go to the bathroom, but I don't
know what I might catch in there."

"Stop! Stop!" I say snorting now because I have the same
need and fear.

Since it's my day to sit on the aisle, I touch Genevieve on
the arm as she passes asking her when we arrive. "Thirty
more minutes. We'll be passing my house soon. I'll come

back and point it out," she says. I look at you and we roll our eyes having heard that about the house yesterday in another country.

"Did she lie about the thirty minutes too?" I whisper.

Because of the luggage rack, you stand, nowhere near your full six foot height, and then move past me bracing against the cold. Bravely leaving your blanket behind, you head to the bathroom. "I'll send care packages," I vow in a low tone.

Soon we arrive at a wonderful inn and are told hot water will be available in the morning. "I know it's wrong of us, but can we be bold Americans and keep each other warm in a cold shower together now?"

"I'm with you," you say.

"I know you're with me, but what about the shower?"

The water in the shower wasn't nearly as cold as the A/C on the bus. Genevieve has left us a form letter announcing when dinner will be served and when to have our luggage outside our rooms in the morning. I whisper that I didn't whisper this much as a child bothering my mother in church.

"Let's eat dinner then make our escape," you suggest.

"Even while it's raining?"

"Because it will always be raining here. It's monsoon season," you joke.

"I love you," I say.

Mischievous you answer, "I'm sorry, forgive me. I thought you were my wife."

"You mean you're not my husband? Thanks for the shower, big guy."

"Nice of you to notice," you say holding an imaginary cigar while your eyebrows impersonate Groucho Marx.

Rain was with us every day of our European trip. But we made it through, learning one important thing: We're good together, even while it's raining.

Indecency

Today, I drove to a bookstore and perused expensive books, gently turning the pages, giving great thought to the quality of the paper and the photography. They were forty and sixty dollar coffee table books about Versailles, about the Windsor's dogs, about the jewelry collection at the Smithsonian. And I reined in my lust for these hardcovers so as to not draw attention. To insure I was not arrested for indecency.

Then I found my way to the poetry section and read of you and me on every page. And wandering through this bookstore, this sea of love, I decided to purchase a sixty-eight page hardback book of oatmeal recipes because oatmeal is your favorite. Stopping by the grocery on the way home, I gathered ingredients for "Oatmeal Scotchies."

After the sun set, you arrived home and said, "Something smells amazing. What did you do today?"

"Visited with Britain's royals, fell in love with you for the first time - over and over – in a little corner of Barstrum's Bookstore - and came home to bake cookies for you. How was Wall Street?"

But by then, you were full of cookie, your eyes were saucers, and your hand was grasping for another. Since it's my job, I said, "You'll ruin your appetite for dinner." And you pulled me to you where I tasted the marvelous blend of you and cookies with a delectably indecent kiss.

Longingly you eyed the open cookie tin, and asked me, "Can I have another?"

I was game and asked you, "Can I?"

This Crazy, Wild Lonely

You loosen my hair that falls past my shoulders. I tilt my head as I remove my earrings. You turn on Willie, turn me on.

I wait…for what? I don't know. Another kiss? One more heartbeat? An assurance of things to come.

Then I give up, give in, remembering how I've walked a stretch of lonely to find you. And tonight belongs to you, to Willie, to Merle, to Toby. "Any song is a good song. Play them all," I assure you as you strive for that right mood not knowing all I want tonight is you. But eventually you take me, make me feel loved like every country song I grew up on.

Another night, a jigger of lonely. I loosen my hair and tilt my head removing my earrings. Walking over to the stereo, I'm wanting one more night in bed with you – no assurances necessary.

I can tell you it was you and not Willie, not Merle, not Toby. But the beer is flat, you've moved on, turned on by another, and damn if I'm not left pacin' rough wooden floors with bare feet. And I'm about to feel sorry for myself, but then Willie starts to sing, and I grab a cold one from the fridge. Listenin' and waitin' for the next man. Lookin' to find a good man on a better stretch of road, someone who'll love me like Willie. Hopin' for a cowboy I can dance with past this crazy, wild lonely. Ready to toss this heartache for a song.

The Magic That Is A Man

I needed to kill a large, floppy, flying insect with long dangly legs that kept swooping down from the ceiling toward my reading lamp. I called my husband into the room.

"What do you need?" he asked. Then swoop past his head. "What the hell?" he shouted, ducking.

"I need you to kill that," I said.

"Sometimes I think that's one of the main reasons you married me – so I would kill insects for you."

"Dear, that's the only reason I married you," I said. Then swoop.

"Damn, that's big," he said not reassuring me at all.

"Try not to mark the walls," I said.

Swoop. BANG!!! – with a rolled magazine. There went the porcelain lamp onto the carpet, cracked, but still on.

"I'm pretty sure I got it." Swoop. BANG!!! "How'd that thing get in here?" Swoop. BANG!!! There went the Russian lacquer boxes flying.

"I think you got it that time, Sweetie," I offered. Swoop. BANG!!! CRASH!!! My favorite Belleek bowl was dead on contact. "This is getting expensive," I observed.

"Do you want it killed or don't you?" he asked.

I knew not to answer. Swoop. "Holy Mother of God!" he yelled. "It won't die!" BAM!!!

Then silence. Not even a swoop. He started looking amid the debris for the carcass because he knew that I'd want proof of its death. "I found it. Over here by the a...what was this, anyway?" he asked.

"An antique jade carving of a Foo Dog," I said trying to be cheerful.

"Well, I didn't mark the walls," he said.

"No, Honey, you didn't. Thank you."

"Need help with anything else?"

I stood looking around at the mass destruction. "Can't think of a thing, Sugar Cakes," I said.

Then suddenly it came to me: the magic that is a man. No jade Foo Dog would ever touch his heart. But he gave up fifteen minutes of a close Pro-football game on TV to come save me and wanted nothing in return, but my love. Well, he had it in spades. My knight would be given a night to remember.

No Having Fun!

My date and I stood in front of the lobster tank. The restaurant had the good intention of allowing us to decide which two lives we would take.

"What about this one that walked over all the others to see you?" Jeffrey, my date, asked.

"Kill a gentleman who came over to say hi? He's special. I couldn't kill that one! Should we buy him and release him back into the wild?!"

"Order three lobsters?"

"How about two lobsters? One to share for dinner, and one to set free?"

My date addressed the mass murderer behind the tank. "Could you please prepare that two-pound lobster over there and save this one in front here for us to take home live?"

"Whatever floats your boat," the man said in a blasé way.

"Jeffrey, I feel so much better. Can we name him?"

"We are setting him free, right?" he asked grabbing my hand as we headed back to our table.

I was in a much better mood about being a party to murder because we were also saving a life. We made quick work of our boiled lobster, and caramel cheesecake. Then we picked up The Gentleman, got in the car and headed for the beach at about nine p.m.

"We're doing a good deed," I said. My date was probably planning on getting lucky after all this. Right then, I couldn't say his hopes were misplaced. "Jeffrey! What do we do with the bands around his claws?! He'll never survive with those on!"

"I've got my Swiss army knife. It has scissors."

"This is the best date!" I said.

"Whatever floats your boat," Jeffrey said purposely mimicking the same deadpan tone of the guy behind the lobster tank.

We soon were standing by the shoreline – the only loving couple on the beach accompanied by their lobster. Now I wasn't so sure we'd done a good thing. Back at the restaurant, The Gentleman would have died a quick death. Now he would have a hard life surviving in the wild. "Jeffrey, wait! Before you cut the claw bands, are we doing the right thing?"

"What do you mean?!" he asked incredulous, up to that point sure we'd be all over each other in bed within the hour.

"He's going to have such a hard life out there. I'm scared for the little guy."

"Nahhh, he'll live forever out there. It's where God intended him to be. He wouldn't have been found in the ocean if he wasn't meant to live there. He'll find a female as pretty as you, and they'll raise little baby lobsters. He has a terrific life ahead of him."

"Since you put it that way, I feel better now. We're doing the right thing." With that, Jeffrey snipped the claw bands and released The Gentleman into the high tide. Jeffrey had made life in the sea sound so good, I said, "Now I wish we could've saved more."

As Jeffrey picked up the bands and put his army knife away, he said, "How many people have ever saved just one life in a lifetime? Not many. I feel good about it, too." Then he added, "But next time, we're going to The Angus Steakhouse, and we're not buying a steer."

"Oh! Can you imagine?!"

"No! We're not imagining. No imagining allowed."

"But..."

"No buying cattle! No!"

"Alright, but wouldn't it be fun if we..."

"No! No having fun!" he said.

Then I started laughing, and he started laughing. And wouldn't you know, we went back to my place and had the time of our lives eating popcorn and watching Billy

Crystal in "City Slickers." It truly was the best date I'd ever been on.

Only, ever since that night, I can't help but think that there's a steer in Amarillo just waiting for Jeffrey and me.

Why Do You Cry...?

I hurry to my lover through a thousand dreams. And in each, I barely find him only to waken and he is gone wherever dreams go.

One night on my way home from work, I glance across the tracks, and there he is, standing on the opposite train platform staring intently at me. As if we've met. As if I belong to him. I want to call to him, but then a train...and he is gone.

After a night of sleep with a hopeful dream about my lover, I get ready early for work and head to the train. There are no seats available, so I stand...next to him. Yes, he's going in my direction. We hold the same metal pole. We smile at one another. I turn to look as a man behind me tugs my winter coat and offers me his seat. I look back at my lover and say over my shoulder, "No thank you. I'm fine." My lover speaks – seemingly knowing my concern of losing him. "Take the seat. I'll move closer." I sit looking up as he smiles down at me. We each begin a sentence, "Where do you...?" Then answer in unison, "The next stop." We step off the train onto a crowded platform. He says, "Take my hand." But he is swallowed by the crowd leaving me grasping the hand of a stranger. My eyes search frantically through a thousand faces to no avail.

The next day, I waken early to catch the same train, to find my lover. But snow and ice on the walkways from last night are slowing down every commuter. As I near the base of the stairs to the platform, I hear the conductor saying, "This train is too full. Make room for the doors to close." The train begins to pull away without me. I'm too late.

As I ascend the stairs to the platform, I begin to cry knowing that I may never see my lover again. It's below freezing. My tears turn to ice on my pink scarf. When I reach the top step – I trip. Only someone catches me, and I look up. It is my lover who has been waiting for me, and says, "Why do you cry when we've been given another chance?"

Sponge

Having quickly become "The Baby" after his birth because Phillip, my husband, wants a Junior and I prefer the name Alex, our young one is now clever enough to unwrap cheesy Baby Belchies and hand them to us to eat. Since I'm no more partial to cheese than The Baby, Phillip has been putting on some cheese-weight of late. As opposed to a beer gut which is a large gut, cheese-weight affects the entire body indiscriminately from what I can tell. Phillip believes "That Baby" is to blame. Now Alex is "That Baby." No, we haven't settled on the name Alex, but I've a plot to teach The Baby his new name in secret and then they'll be no going back. The Baby's with me on this or so he initially led me to believe.

Phillip's name is on The Baby's birth certificate. And so my husband feels that this gives him the right to call The Baby by that name. But because my husband and I can't agree on a name, The Baby has been without a name for about two years and unfortunately has settled on his own name: "SpongeBob." I don't find this amusing because Alex really doesn't own rights to his own cartoon and "Bob" makes me think of a woman's hairdo.

Every time I call The Baby, Alex, in my mind I'm thinking "Phillip" because we're engaged in a skirmish and that's who I'm fighting against. So it was inevitable. The other day I sweetly and in a sing-songy way called Phillip, "Alex" by mistake and the jig was up. My husband became angry, and I said, "Look, The Baby doesn't care for Alex anymore than you. I give up. You'd think twenty-four hours in labor would have earned me some rights." That's when Phillip blew up.

"That Baby will be the end of us!" he yelled as he got ready to take The Baby out in his stroller.

Well, we're walking down Fifth Avenue somewhere in the sixties. In his stroller, The Baby is glowing in a yellow fuzzy mohair sweater, and is holding his arms extended on both sides to catch the breeze. The sun is out. It's a fall day full of possibilities.

A well-appointed older woman stops us and says, "What a wonderful child! He's precious! What's his name?"

"SpongeBob," says The Baby.

Laughing she says, "And so brilliant!"

My husband is beaming. I'm beaming. SpongeBob gives a thumbs-up sign with each hand. Maybe his peers will think he's got a cool name. Actually, it is brilliant because he's got to be the only child in the whole world with that name. I just hope everyone won't shorten it to Sponge. Now, that'd be no name at all, would it?

Sundays At Six

You can hear it coming in from the cliffs. Every Sunday at six, he plays. He knows the romance of bagpipes. But when I go to see where and who, the direction of the music changes leading me astray. So I've never seen him. But I love him for his music. Makes me long for a time before this one, when my skirts graced my ankles and I had all day to make lace by hand.

I think the ocean leads to confusion, making my search nearly impossible. But the breeze has become a friend, and most Sundays I hear the entire song for that evening carried the quarter mile to me from the cliffs.

Weeks ago, I devised a plan to crochet antique threads in intricate patterns around rocks. I write love poems that I wrap in plastic wrap to lie beneath my threads. Every Saturday I place more of them along the cliffs...hoping. I check each Monday morning to see if they've been disturbed. It's my only way to reach him. I haven't made plans if someone else should come upon them. I've simply written beneath the poems, "Please return this note to 5 Hunthill Road. Please ring the bell."

The music continues to penetrate my shingled home near the water, to penetrate me. I live for my Sundays at six. I wonder if he's married, or single and shy. Anyone who plays with such emotion must surely know of love.

Today, there was no breeze and I went out searching for him at six. This time the closer I got to the cliff, the more I was sure of his direction. The bagpipes were never lovelier than when I came nearer and nearer to them. I decided to take the stairs to the beach and follow the base of the cliffs, looking up as I walked. Excited, I thought he was at the top of the cliff on the other side of a rocky protrusion, playing for my soul alone to hear.

But there, on top of the cliff, was a woman of about fifty, her red hair grayed from age, playing the bagpipes. And the music changed. No longer romantic, no longer played for me, but laughing at me. Ashamed of my foolishness and that my heart had led me astray, I turned and headed home, my lips trembling, warm tears falling onto my silk blouse, my hands in fists as I hurried. A breeze picked up and the music kept pace with me. All I wanted then was to be inside my home away from the world…alone.

I'd been deceived. Humiliated. What a fool I'd been to love. What a fool I'd been to dream. And tonight after the music dies, I will go to the cliff's edge and destroy what remains of my love before my plan is found out. I shall never love another. They'll find me and think I simply slipped.

Three

The cool Georgia rain hitting early autumn's hot tin rooves created ghosts that floated skyward. But we were too busy to see. Alone. Just us two. In a bed that could have been any size as long as you were above me. Then we'd shower and make love again and again over the course of two days. I kept pressing my finger into your cleft chin committing you to memory. Those eyes...your eyes that crinkled with your every smile, I wanted them to always be happy and never see the horrors where you were headed. But that was our unspoken desire.

Too soon you were dressed in your uniform. I wanted to undress you and rewind forty-eight hours. You held me so long upon leaving that I thought you might stay. We never talked of love. But when you held my face with both of your hands and looked into my eyes, searching, memorizing, yearning...it was then you spoke of love. Not with words, but with your entire being. Good-bye came too soon. I stood in the street watching your car drive away, even as the torrential rain obstructed my view.

I took cover inside where I was left with memories everywhere. The flowers you brought resting in a vase on the kitchen table, a desolate shower, the bed – unkempt. All no longer mine, but yours. Each yours. I slept on those sheets for days until it became too sad a tribute. It was in this way I began my life again. Every moment at war with your war. I became too well-versed in the fragility of things.

You forgot your cologne. I wore it every day after. I purchased your brand of shampoo. You couldn't tell me where you were going, so I believed you were still with me. I built my life around those two days. I still buy the same brand of coffee, and drink from the same two mugs.

I wanted you to know that despite an ocean separating us, we're together in a world that could be any size as long as I'm in your heart. Because he's one month now. And even though I don't know where you are, you're with me. Come home soon. He has your eyes.

As If The Gods Weren't Laughing

We danced, strolled, dined out, dined in, took the high road. I listened, nurtured, spoke up, supported me by supporting you. You encouraged, stood by, walked your talk.

So for our anniversary, I promised myself we would do the unusual for us. We would go white water rafting, or visit the Grand Canyon, maybe fly over glaciers in Alaska by helicopter. Or stay in bed, as always, in our pajamas, the floor strewn with newspapers in several languages, too engrossed in our reading to each other to fill the water carafes on our nightstands. If you prefer we could sleep until one p.m. and think hard about getting out of bed during the three hours that follow. Then we should shower...together. But only if you prefer.

Maybe we make a week of it – our anniversary. Or what do you say to a month? Not in bed all of the time. People would talk. Journalists would come and take photos, you know.

How many years now? How many decisions as paths forked leading to more paths? And we're each still here. No surprise really. Thus my idea of the glaciers or water rafting. Make memories. Make new friends. Make sure we unplug the toaster before we leave.

Or, if you prefer, we could build a fire, turn down the A/C, and relax in our overstuffed chairs. I'd write you love notes. You'd write your articles. Our only needs a loving, telling gaze and one finger to stroke a cheek.

I'd suggest you think about it, only I know your decision now like I know your favorite shirt, that you favor soft jazz, that the outdoors makes you crazy. This anniversary, we'll stay in. You'll write and I'll make our favorite pasta. Our day will pass leisurely. And when night arrives we'll vow to spend another year, another decade, another lifetime with each other as if it was entirely our game...as if the Gods weren't laughing at our hubris.

Pish Tosh

Our eyes return to one another, at times discovering something new, and other times filled with a gladness to come upon the old. Our hearing is going, but not our humor.

"You're going to sea taken by Ahab?" I asked.

"No, I'm going to be takin' a nap."

Thirty minutes later, he walked through the kitchen. I said, "How's your nap going?"

"Ahab never showed," he said matter-of-factly continuing on his way through the house on a mission. We smiled, each of us knowing we were living longer than the end according to insurance charts.

The next day, he walked inside and said, "The beetles are coming on."

"Good. I've always enjoyed them," I said.

"What are you talking about?" he asked.

"What are you talking about?" I asked.

"Japanese beetle bugs," he said.

"Does that mean we won't be hearing music?"

"Only if we turn on the stereo," he said.

"I get it, but hopefully no one is listening to this conversation."

"Hopefully for you, you mean. I've known what it was about from the start," he grumbled.

"Only because you started this time," I said.

"Pish tosh," he said rummaging through the junk drawer. It was always pish tosh when I'd made a good point against him.

Two days later, he said, "Heavy metal always gives me pause to think."

"I become pensive with Bartok," I said.

"Where are you now?" he asked perplexed.

"Well, I can't stand heavy metal, but I like Bartok if I'm in the right mood."

"I was talking about scrap."

"No that's rap, Dear, and heavy metal is not rap," I said sure I was on the correct course.

"There's a heavy metal junk heap on the other side of town. I'd like to make a sculpture," he said.

"I see! Wouldn't you need an acetylene torch?"

"Not with you as my flame," he said surprising me. He could do that – make me sigh.

Then yesterday, I asked, "You're going to Bangkok to fry lightening words today?"

"No," he said patiently, "I'm going to bang the wok to try frightening birds away."

But today, I was very proud of myself. When I didn't understand him, I simply said, "I'm sorry. What did you say?"

To which he responded with love, "What did you hear?"

Blue-Tinged Snow In Winter 1982

Your opened envelope and letter are stained blue due to the snow they tumbled across as the wind and I chased them down halfway across a field. Until that moment, you wrote of our friendship last summer and when you began to love me. You mentioned you were subletting in Paris alone and thinking of me. "Please come" was written there.

At the moment the wind decided to take them from me, I saw your address had been neatly written at the bottom of the letter, and top of the envelope – now abstract paintings that I carefully dried and keep in the top pocket of my jean jacket, checking each day to see if the words have since become legible. The only word I can decipher is "love." Every day, I do as it commands.

Foolish, I went back to that area of the field hoping your words might be written there. But you are lost in blue-tinged snow, and now, so too am I.

ALPHABETICAL ORDER

www.ingramcontent.com/pod-product-compliance
Lightning Source LLC
Chambersburg PA
CBHW060623130626
46555CB00002B/636